BAD BART'S
REVENGE

Advanced Reader

Written by Gary Harbo

Illustrated by
Gary Harbo and Shawn Wallace

KUTIE KARI BOOKS, INC.

BAD BART'S
REVENGE

Advanced Reader

ISBN 1-884149-03-0

To receive a free brochure write:
Kutie Kari Books, Inc.
2461 Blueberry St.
Inver Grove Hts., MN 55076

To place your order call:
1-800-395-8843
Mon-Fri 8am-5pm Central Time
Visa/Mastercard

Revenge

Revenge is sweet, or so they say;
But what have you accomplished, on that fateful day?

You've stooped to the level, of the one that hurt you;
To this burning fire, you've added a dangerous fuel.

Now you're locked in a battle, that no one can win;
It's a downward spiral, that you'll find yourself in!

For every act can be met, with a counter more severe;
Until the original problem is lost, in a battle of mirrors.

For when you get your revenge, it is commonly found;
That you've reflected onto yourself, another vicious round.

Revenge doesn't work, it's been proven many times before;
Solving the problem, is the only key to that door!

Forget revenge and find the key.........

Gary Harbo

"Hey Bart!" Slimey the Snake said in a teasing way. "How's my big mummy doing? Are you feeling a little better today? Here, let me honk your nose again."

"Slimey, knock it off! My nose is feeling a lot better, but if you touch it one more time, I'm going to make a belt out of you! I swear I will," Bart growled in reply.

"Okay, okay," Slimey said. "Bart, you don't have to get so huffy about it. You're lucky to have a nose at all, after that radical roll you took on your skateboard. I really don't believe skateboards are meant to have rockets on them. I guess maybe now you'll think twice before gluing rockets on your skateboard again.

By the way, when did Doc say the bandages were coming off?"

1

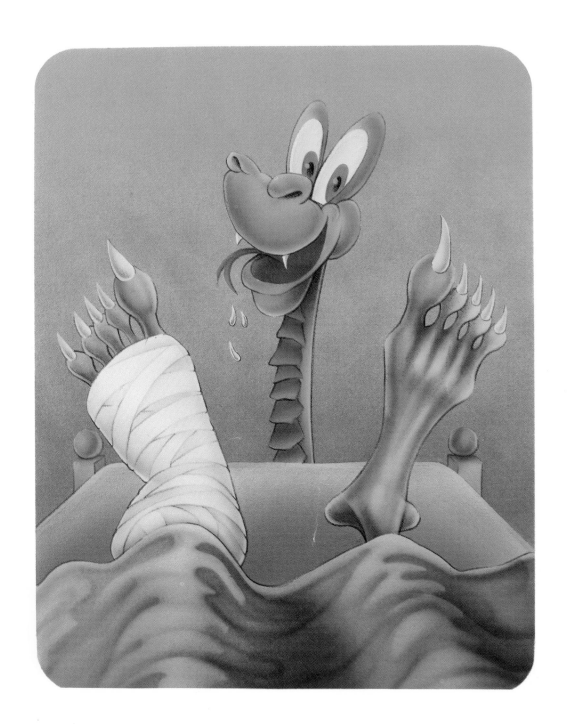

2

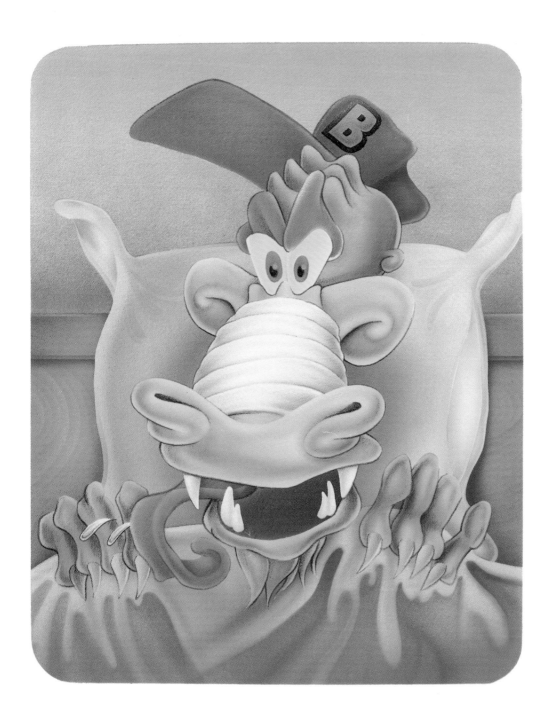

3

"He's supposed to take these things off tomorrow," Bart said to the snake. "Man, as soon as that happens, I'm going to be on the move again. It feels like I've been cooped-up in here forever."

"Good deal," said Slimey. "Maybe then we can go into Lynd and play. How about if we get on your skateboard, cruise on over to the playground and shoot some hoops? I'd like to see if I can still beat you in basket-ball. Of course with your bad foot and all, now you'll have a natural excuse."

"Listen, Slimey," Bart shouted, "You could never beat me in basketball. You're terrible on defense. You can't even put a hand in my face. Besides, I don't have time for fun. I have to find Kari and Herby and make them pay for what they have done! This whole hospital trip was their fault!"

4

"Whoa, Dude!" Slimey exclaimed. "Excuse me, Bart, but don't you remember what caused your big curb scene? I hate to be a stickler for details, but I believe it was you that was chasing them. It wasn't Herby and Kari's fault your rockets blasted off. In fact, you have no one to blame but yourself! You never should have been trying to chase them in the first place."

"Don't be such a smart-alec snake," Bart mumbled in reply. "So what if I was chasing them? Do you think I care who's fault it was? My rockets are broken, my skateboard is out of commission, my beautiful body is all beat up and I've been cooped-up in this hospital forever! Someone has got to pay!" Bart roared.

"Bart," Slimey replied. "You'll have to learn how to control that temper, dude. You'll never make any friends if you continue to be so rude."

Bart snarled, "I don't care about making friends. Who needs them anyway? Friends will just let you down. I'll tell you what, Slimey, in my book you only need one to play."

"Man, that's a nasty attitude you have," Slimey quickly said. "Come on, Bart, why don't you forget about this revenge nonsense? I bet Kari and Herby would be willing to forget all about the past. They're really pretty cool kids. I bet they'd even be willing to play some ball with us."

"Just pipe down, Slimey," Bart snarled in reply. "I want to get back to the matter at hand. While you were rambling on, I just came up with a brilliant plan. As soon as I get these bandages off, we'll track Herby down like a dog. Then I'll sneak up from behind and wrestle him to the ground like a hog."

8

The next day, as Doc took Bart's bandages off he said, "I hope this taught you to cool your jets, Bart. You should be thankful that Herby and Kari brought you in here."

"Yah right, Doc," Bart said as he rolled his eyes. Then Bart looked in the mirror and said, "Man, I look great."

Slimey laughed to himself, "If he's waiting for me to agree with him, he'll have a long, long wait."

"Wipe that smile off your face, Slimey," for Bart had seen him out of the corner of his eye. "I'm the best looking one in here, and that's no lie."

"Right," Slimey laughed. "Come on superstar, let's go get some fresh air before you lose all of your senses."

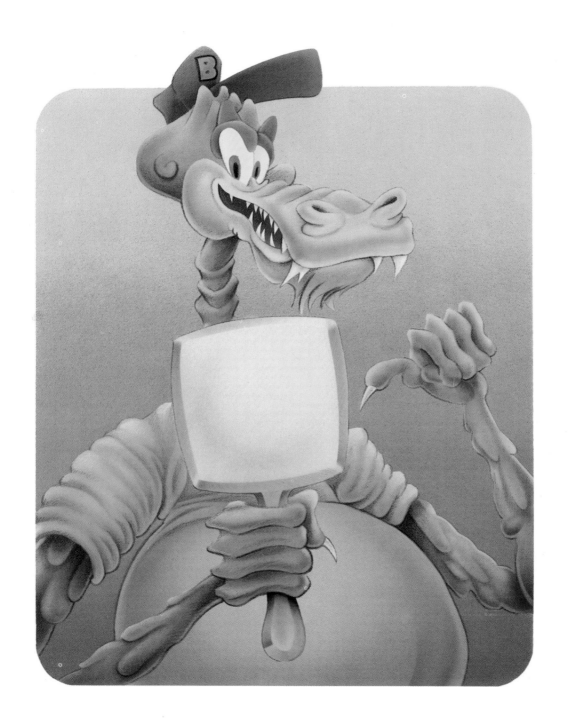

After leaving the hospital, Bart decided to go over to the playground and see if they could find Kari and Herby. As they came to the field, Bart whispered, "Hey, Slimey, this is our big chance. Look over at the basketball hoop. Are those friends of Herby and Kari?"

"Yesssss," Slimey hissed. "It's Brittany and Brandon. Looks like they're shooting a game of hoops. Hey, Brittany has a pretty darn nice hook-shot."

"I could snuff them both out in basketball," Bart snarled. "You obviously don't remember me in action, Slimey. Unfortunately, I don't have time to teach them a thing or two about the game. I'm on a mission!"

"Come on Bart, haven't you ever heard that revenge never solves any problem? Even I know that!" Slimey said as they sneaked up on the two.

12

"Shhhhh!" Bart said. "I don't need the advice of a snake. Now be quiet. I'm trying to hear what Brandon and Brittany have to say."

"Did you hear that Bad Bart wiped out on his skateboard?" Brittany asked. "Thank goodness he's okay. I heard that just before he rolled in the grass, it looked like he was trying to do a wild dance along the curb. I bet that was a wild sight. I can imagine how frightened he must have been when he saw those rockets come blasting off his skateboard."

"Man, I wish I could have seen his face," Brandon laughed in reply. "It must have been a radical sight to see Big Bart on the fly!"

"Come on, Slimey! I've heard enough of this garbage!" Bart angrily said.

13

14

15

As they sneaked up behind Brandon, Bart was angry enough to burst. When he gets in that mood, you can always expect the worst. Unfortunately, Brittany and Brandon didn't have a clue that Bart was in the bushes. As Bart approached Brandon, Brittany gulped in fear and tried to warn him, but it was too late.

Bart tapped Brandon on the shoulder and said, "Listen you little mutt, if you don't tell me where Kari and Herby are, I just might do that wild dance on your head!"

"He means it, Brandon and Brittany," Slimey said. "Ever since his skateboard accident, he hasn't exactly been a happy camper. Of course, Bart is always in a bad mood. In fact, I think he was born with that nasty look on his face. Isn't that right Bart? You're never happy about anything! Did the doctor drop you on the floor when you were born? Is that your problem? I bet you slipped right out of her hands, and she dropped you flat on your snout! Come on Bart, you can let it out."

"Slimey, would you be quiet!" Bart quickly snapped. "Man, sometimes I don't have the foggiest idea where you're coming from."

He then turned to Brittany and Brandon and growled, "You may think my swan dive in the grass was funny, but since you weren't there, I'll forgive you. If you want to continue your game of basketball, however you had better tell me where Kari and Herby are playing."

"Hey, we're sorry dude," Brittany quickly said. "We didn't mean to get down on you, but after all, you were the one that caused the big accident. They weren't chasing you!"

"Besides, revenge is wrong, Bart," Brandon said with a nervous voice.

"Say, what!" Bart roared in reply. "Are you trying to tell me that I'm making the wrong choice?"

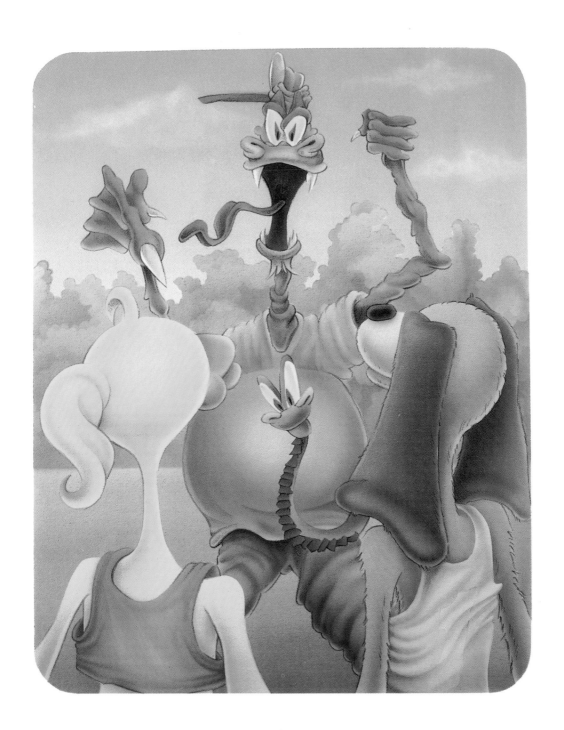

18

"How dare these kids talk to me about right and wrong," Bart said to himself. "All I wanted to know was where to find Kari and Herby. But nooooo, they have to tell me how I should act. Well, I don't care what they think. If I wanted a do-gooder opinion, I'd talk to Slimey the Snake."

Bart was ready to jump into action, because his patience had certainly run low. Brittany and Brandon could see how consumed Bart was on getting revenge, and they began to get a little anxious.

Along came Tattletale Turkey who gobbled, "They're down at the ball diamond, Bart. Now don't forget who told you so."

"Thanks, Tattletale. You're a real tur-key," Bart laughed to himself.

Now that Bart had his information, he was quickly on his way. He could sense that he would soon be getting what he so richly deserved.

"You're lucky Tattletale is more of a stool pigeon than a turkey," Bart said to Brittany and Brandon, as he left with Slimey the Snake. "Now it's time to visit Kari and Herby. Just think of the surprise that we'll make. Come on Slimey, I feel like playing some ball."

"Leave them alone!" Brandon yelled to Big Bad Bart. "They haven't done anything to you. For once in your life, why don't you play it smart?"

"Go back to your basketball game," Slimey turned and said to the two. "Bart has to get this out of his system. There isn't anything you can do."

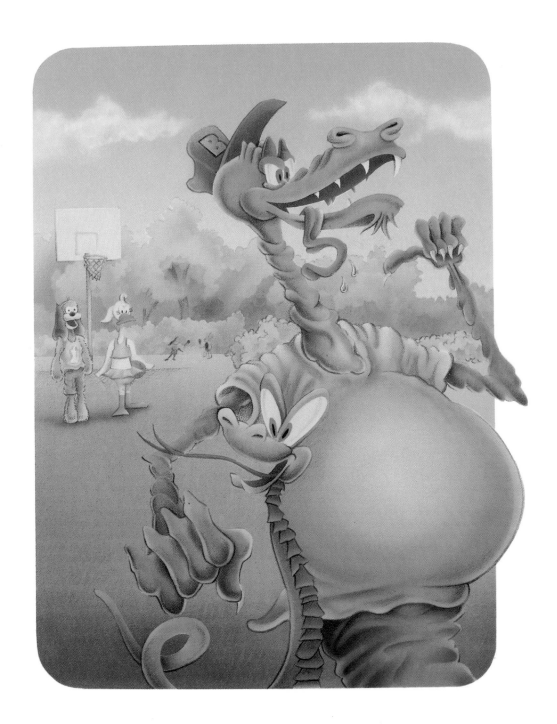

Sure enough, down at the ball diamond Kari and Herby were in the middle of a good game of baseball. Kari was batting and Herby had just pitched the ball. As the ball came over the plate Kari swung as hard as she could, and you could hear the crack of her bat several blocks away.

"This is excellent!" Kari said, as she watched her long hit go towering towards the outfield wall. "Hey, Herby, let's see you catch up with that one."

"Wow!" Herby said to himself. "Kari can really hit that ball a country mile. I have to make tracks if I'm going to run that ball down."

Meanwhile, Bart heard the commotion and was hustling up to the fence. Maybe this was the opportunity he was looking for.

Everyone knew that Herby was fast and could run like a deer. It only took a couple of seconds before he was on track to catch the ball as it reached the top of its flight. Little did he know that Bad Bart was peeking over the fence and licking his chops at the sight.

"Slimey, this is my lucky day," Bart said, drooling with delight. "Herby doesn't have a clue that we are here. I think we should give the kid a double play. Ha, Ha, Ha."

"Yessss, I would say it's looking pretty dim for Herby," Slimey hissed in reply. "Boy is he going to be shocked when he sees the two of us in his face!"

"Come on Slimey," Bart said to his sidekick. "Let's jump the fence."

Herby stopped in his tracks as his feet dug a deep trench. He wasn't going to catch that ball, not with those two ugly heads coming at him from over the fence.

"Hello, Herby," Bart roared. "You sure are looking fine. I can't tell you how good it is to see you. I've been dreaming of this for a long, long time."

"Yah right, Bart," Herby said, "and I'm Kirby Puckett of the Minnesota Twins......"

"I don't know if you're Kirby," Slimey laughed. "But you probably will be a puck in a second."

"Somehow I doubt it guys," Herby smiled in reply. "Judging from my calculations, I believe you're about to catch Kari's fly. Heads-up everyone!"

Bart thought it was a trick and wasn't about to look up. He knew how fast Herby was and wasn't about to let him get away.

Owww!" Bart howled as his eyes opened wide in pain. "What in the world was that, a run away train?"

Sure enough, Kari's ball came down right where Herby thought it would land. Bart's dreams of revenge suddenly ended in a brilliant flash. The baseball had fallen from the sky and landed with a resounding crash.

He quickly found out the hard way as to why Herby had been racing towards the fence. Kari's long fly ball had nailed Bart right on the top of his head. It rattled his teeth and shook the back of his eyelids. Like a big old redwood tree that is about to go down, Bart wobbled around and then crashed to the ground.

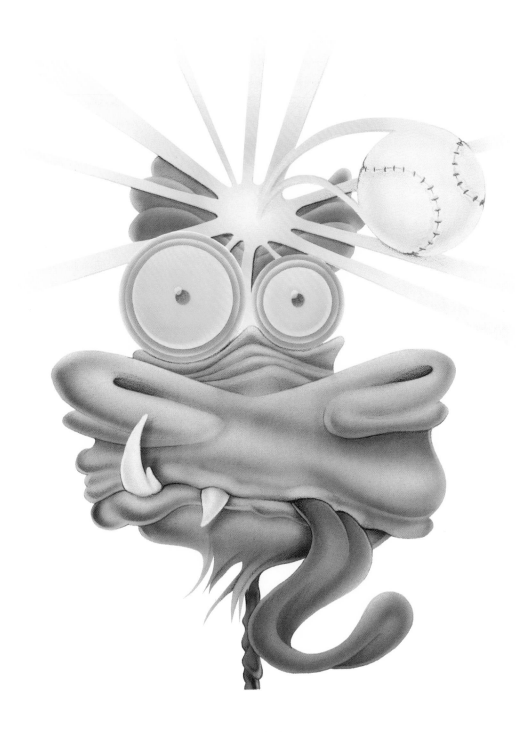

30

Bart didn't even know what hit him as he fell to the ground. A strange smile seemed to come to his face, as he heard the distant music of birds singing in the air. As he lay there in a daze, he began to think that maybe revenge really wasn't so sweet after all.

Old Slimey was on the move, for he wasn't about to stick around. He didn't want to be anywhere near this angry dragonator when he woke up. He quickly slid into the bushes, leaving Bart sprawled out on the ground. It's amazing how fast that snake could move when he felt the need to.

"I told him that revenge was bad," Slimey tried to explain. "Maybe now old sleeping beauty will change his ways."

Kari had seen the whole thing from where she had hit the ball. When she saw that Herby was in trouble, she began to hustle out to the field.

As Herby turned around and saw her coming up to him he said, "Nice hit, Kari! You sure stopped Bart in his tracks. I can't get over the look on his face when that ball bonked him on the top of his head. Wow, what a play!"

"Let's go help him get up," Kari said. "Maybe it's time we find out why old Bart always has such an attitude. Let's try and find out why he seems to be so mean to everyone in general."

"You're right, Kari," Herby said. "Maybe we should try to give him a hand. Who knows, maybe someday we can even teach him how to be a friend. Let's go help him get up."

THE END

Gary Harbo grew up in Lynd, a small rural community in Southwestern, Minnesota. He founded KUTIE KARI BOOKS, Inc. in 1990 and now lives in the St. Paul area. Gary's books and cartoon characters were inspired by his love and appreciation for his children, Kari (14) and Gary II (13).

As an author and illustrator, Gary teaches art lessons to over 25,000 elementary school children every year. His motivational talks encompass the whole process of writing, illustrating and publishing. His talks include; Keynote speaker for the International Reading Association, Chapter One Parent/Children Workshops, guest author for Southwest and Northeast Minnesota Young Authors Conferences, Rotary Club motivational talks, as well as Author-in-Residence for hundreds of schools in seven different states.

His love of drawing began at an early age and has resulted in several first place finishes in art competitions for his colored pencil illustrations. His work is mostly in wildlife and cartooning.

Gary graduated with high honors from South Dakota School of Mines and Technology (SDSM&T) in 1983 with a B.S. in Electrical Engineering. During his senior year at SDSM&T, Gary's interest in children spawned his original design of a Crib Death Detector. He created this invention for his newborn daughter, Kari. It won him national acclaim with a 2nd place finish in the Institute of Electrical and Electronic Engineering finals in Houston, Texas.

In 1983 Gary accepted a management position at US West Communications and spent 8 years developing marketing systems in Aberdeen, SD., Omaha, NE., Phoenix, AZ and Minneapolis, MN. His creative design of the first-of-its-kind Market Intelligence System culminated in his reception of a US West Communications Presidential award in 1991.

In March of 1991, Gary resigned from his analytical career to pursue his lifelong dream of working with children. His Minnesota based company, KUTIE KARI BOOKS Inc., has published five exciting picture books, **My New Friend**, **Bad Bart's Revenge**, **Bart Becomes a Friend**, **The Great Train Ride** and **The Black Hills Adventure**. These action-packed adventures are bringing smiles to tens of thousands of children across the Midwest.

For more information on ordering books or receiving information on school visits, write or call:

KUTIE KARI BOOKS, Inc.
2461 Blueberry St.
Inver Grove Heights, MN 55076
612-450-7427 or 1-800-395-8843

Bart and His Circle of Friends